THE MINECRAFT LEGEND: The Beginning BOOK #1

By Michael Rios

Ages 7-12

THE LEGENDS OF MINECRAFT SERIES

TABLE OF CONTENTS

Chapter 1: How Everything Started
Chapter 2: The Discovery of Notch
Chapter 3: The Chamber
Chapter 4: Sinister Plots
Chapter 5: Steve's Plan
Chapter 6: Jungle Beasts
Chapter 7: Notch is Back
Chapter 8: Showdown
Extra: Afterward…

CHAPTER 1:
How Everything Started

A very long time ago, before
Minecraft had a name, two players named
Jeb and Notch were underground mining for
diamonds. They were near the bedrock
layer, about forty blocks under the surface.
"Jeb, I found gold," said Notch. Jeb looked
at Notch. "Where did you find it?" Jeb
asked.

"Somewhere over here," said Notch.
Jeb broke some gold ore and fell into an
abandoned mineshaft. "What is this place?"
Jeb asked. He has never been in a mineshaft
before. This was all new to him. Gold, iron,
and mineshafts. Notch jumped down. "This
place is old. It's been here before us," said
Notch. As they walked, they looked around.

A zombie appeared at the corner.
"Careful Jeb!" cried Notch. The zombie hit

Jeb, and began bleeding on his face. Notch took out his pickaxe and threw it at the zombie, clobbering its face and destroying it. "Are you okay?" asked Notch. "We should invent swords and food," replied Jeb. As they walked, a cave spider appeared in front of them.

"Look out!" yelled Jeb. The cave spider bit Notch and Notch was poisoned. Jeb hit the spider in the face, shattering its fangs. The spider hit Jeb's face where he was bleeding, and Jeb cried out in pain.

Jeb threw the pickaxe at the spider and the spider vanished. Notch got up, with his health low. "We are going to invent swords," said Notch. They mined for diamonds, and Notch took a stick and two diamonds and made the very first sword in Minecraft history, the most powerful diamond sword.

"This should protect us," said Jeb as he crafted one too. Suddenly, there was an explosion behind Jeb. "What was that?"

asked Jeb. "A green figure with four tiny rectangular feet," replied Notch. Then, something serious happened. A zombie followed by a creeper approached them. "Is the tiny green one with no arms friendly?" asked Jeb. "Oh… I don't think so. RUN!" cried Notch. "We have swords!" shouted Jeb, ignoring Notch. Jeb charged at the zombie and the creeper exploded, destroying the zombie.

Jeb was now even lower on health. "We should add bows and arrows," said Notch. He mined gravel; got a feather from a chicken he destroyed earlier, and got a stick. He made four arrows. "Now we need to make a bow," said Notch, but then, a creeper exploded behind him and he disappeared. "Notch…? Notch!" cried Jeb.

Jeb could not find his friend. All he saw was abandoned items on the ground. He picked them up, went to the surface, and walked to their house. Notch wasn't there. All Jeb saw was a book lying on Notch's bed. He read the book with interest.

It read: *Jeb, I have lost track of you. I don't remember anything after I blew up. I have no idea were I am. But what I know is: I have teleported this book to my bed. This is what I want you to know: I am lost in the vast thick of a jungle near this old cobblestone temple. It is filled with moss and cobwebs are everywhere. I cannot find my way back. Please find me soon-signed Notch.* Jeb felt like sobbing. He wanted to bring Notch back.

He had no idea what to do… so years past and Jeb could not find Notch. But, then cities began appearing with villagers, and some new brave players were born.

CHAPTER 2:
The Discovery of
Notch

Forty years later, a player named Steve was born. He was an incredibly brave player. He grew up in a large village, regarded as the Ultimate City of Minecraft. No one knew who the first players were, so it was a secret. Steve was really good at PvP. He started taking PvP classes if he found himself in a battle. He was one of the greatest players that ever fought in tournaments.

When Steve was about thirty years old, he started to wonder about who the first players in Minecraft history. He wanted to know so badly, so he asked everyone in town. No one knew, so he went to the library. He took out a book that was written by a villager named John.

He read John's book and learned information that one of the first players was named Jeb. Steve wondered if Jeb was alive. On his computer, he checked the location of Jeb, and discovered Jeb was deep underground in a stronghold. Steve started to get worried. They're rumors that hostile mobs locked players up in jail cells inside strongholds to rot.

He planned an adventure to find Jeb and asked him who the very first player in Minecraft history was. Although this might sound crazy, Steve's mind was filled with adventures. He fought well; he took classes on pickaxes and how to use them, and even took classes for caving.

He started to head out. But when he started to go, it was already night time and hostile mobs came out from everywhere. A large pack of creepers appeared. Steve realized he wasn't prepared to take on hostile mobs. He began mining down, into the ground. He had a map and found Jeb's location. The map showed that Jeb was on the eastside, so Steve headed that direction.

A few miles away, at a temple, an army of hostile mobs were planning something very evil. Herobrine was in charge. "We are going to make serious havoc, so careful not to destroy yourselves," Herobrine said in a strong and loud tone. "Keep an eye out for Iron Golems, Snow Golems, players, wolves and ocelots. The creepers will go into the desert and destroy any enemies," continued Herobrine.

"Zombies, you and your general will hunt down villagers and take prisoners. Skeletons, you go in the Jungle and make sure no one goes into any temples. Spiders, you go into the mesa biome and guard the secret chamber along with the cave spiders. Slimes go into the swamp and help witches destroy enemies. Witches go into mineshafts and guard the cave spiders. Cave spiders, you heard your assignment earlier. Go to the chamber. Remember: the chamber is where the herobrine warriors are preparing for the destruction of the Overworld. Do not let anyone in except for us. Our main goal is to find the creator of Minecraft!" Herobrine commanded as he finished his battle speech. The monsters and the hostile army ran off, obeying their boss.

Far away, as Steve broke the ground, he ran into a mineshaft. He looked around for strongholds, just in case. As he walked, an army of witches appeared and threw as many potions at Steve. Steve was willing to get away, but a witch blocked him. Quickly, they surrounded Steve and tossed harmful potions at him from all directions. Steve drank a potion of invisibility and disappeared.

"Close one," said Steve, as he banged his pickaxe. Suddenly, an explosion went off behind him. A herobrine warrior appeared. "You have come to the right place, victim. Our master is going to destroy the Overworld!" said the Herobrine warrior. More witches appeared behind the herobrine warrior. "Not if I can help it!" said Steve as he swiftly jumped, and did a spin in the air, with his diamond sword pointed at them. With a lot of force, Steve struck a witch, destroying one.

The herobrine warrior took out a herobrine sword and twirled it in the air. He hit Steve, and Steve fell to the ground. "You don't seem so tough," said the warrior. He struck Steve on the back, making Steve bleed. Steve got up and hit the white-eyed warrior on the face. "That's all you got?!" yelled the warrior. He hurt Steve on the arm, and Steve cried out in pain.

"You are defeated," said the warrior. Steve fell to the ground, with anger cursing through him. He got up, slicing the herobrine warrior on the arm. "Oh no, you don't!" said the warrior, getting ready to hit Steve. Steve was ready this time, and jumped on time when the warrior attempted to hit Steve.

The herobrine warrior missed Steve, and Steve hit the warrior on the back. The herobrine warrior got up and threw cobwebs on Steve, making him stand in place. The warrior hit Steve all around, and Steve's health was extremely low. He got a bucket of water and poured it on the cobwebs, destroying them. Steve advanced the warrior, and slammed into the warrior like a bison.

"Seriously! I will show you," said the warrior. Steve was ready for his next move. As the warrior sprinted with his diamond sword pointed at him, Steve jumped in the air and dodged the warrior attack. Then, Steve hit the warrior and the warrior was destroyed.

Tired, Steve took the warriors items. But then, he saw a book that the warrior had. He took it and it read: *This is a reminder for all herobrine warriors and hostile mobs: we are taking over the Overworld and turning it into a new world called: Hostileworld. Destroy everything in you path that you find it to be trouble, and you will be okay. We are going to destroying the creator of*

Minecraft: Notch- Sincerely, Herobrine, the boss. Steve looked at the cover. It said: The Destruction of the Overworld.

CHAPTER 3:
The Chamber

Steve didn't feel safe that he had gone out by himself with hostile mobs on the prowl, so he decided to go back to the surface and warn the village. But then, more witches appeared a few blocks away. Steve didn't have time to fight; he had to save the village. He ran away from the witches, into a cave. As Steve looked around, he heard a flow of water nearby, and he thought it was a good sign.

When he walked to the water, he saw a dungeon with cave spiders. He quickly hid behind a stone wall, and he could hear the spiders talking. "He must warn our boss. I heard voices coming from the mine," one of the spiders hissed. "What if they are just herobrine warriors and we don't have anything to worry about," the second spider hissed. "Calm down! I think I saw a username on the other side of that wall," said the third spider.

Steve realized that was him. He quickly escaped, getting away with it. He heard something about the cave spiders 'warning their boss,' and Steve thought that might be Herobrine. As he ran, he heard footsteps that echoed through the cave walls like a great drop of water. "Who is there?" asked Steve, quietly. There was no response. Then, an arrow flew by.

"Don't shoot!" cried Steve, nervously. Another arrow flew past and struck Steve. Steve ran as fast as he could, hoping to get away from the arrows. Another arrow struck him, and he started to bleed. Steve put on his armor, and took out his diamond sword. He sprinted were the arrows went, and found someone with a Bow and Arrow. Steve struck him until the guy was at four in health. "Stop! Stop! Please stop striking me," cried the guy, begging.

"How can I trust you?!" yelled Steve. "You shot dozens of arrows hitting me, and every single one hit me!" said Steve striking the guy again. "I'll give you a diamond," begged the guy. Steve wanted a diamond to make a pickaxe, so he took the guy's diamond.

"What is your name?" asked Steve. "My name is Henry, and I think your name is BartingGuest?" asked Henry. "What!?" asked Steve. "You username appears to be glitched. It says *BartingGuest*," said Henry, chuckling. "Barting isn't a real word. Are you sure?" said Steve. A sinister witch-like laugh could be heard through the cave as it echoed.

"We better get going. This place is invested with witches," said Henry. "I noticed. A monster named Herobrine is planning on destroying the Overworld and renaming it 'Hostileworld'," said Steve. "Horrible name," said Henry. As they mined up, Steve remembered about Jeb.

"Have you heard about Jeb?" asked Steve. "No. Who is he?" replied Henry. "One of the first players in Minecraft" responded Steve. "Notch, he was the first player in Minecraft," Steve continued. "You know the very first player?!" cried Henry, surprised. "Whatever," said Steve. As they reached the surface, they found themselves in the desert. "Oh no…Bad sign," said Henry. "How do you know?" asked Steve. "There is nothing out here," said Henry. "They are desert villages," said Steve.

Night time came quickly, and suddenly an army of creepers followed by a herobrine warrior appeared. Steve saw them. "Run!" Steve yelled. Henry turned and saw a sea of green followed by a warrior racing toward them. "Oh god," said Henry, and his face turned pale. Something about seeing all those creepers was hypnotizing, and he wanted to watch. "There's no time!" yelled Steve. He grabbed Henry's arm and pulled it back. The herobrine warrior threw ignited TNT in front of them and it exploded, making a large hole.

They were blocked. "You will be taken prisoner," said the warrior. The stampede of creepers came to a sudden stop.

"Search them," demanded the warrior. Two creepers went to them to take their weapons, with weird robot arms Steve never seen before. "Take them with us and alert Herobrine," said the warrior. Four creepers with mechanical arms took them, with Steve's and Henry's hands on their backs.

Then, Steve saw they were headed toward a canyon. It separated the desert with the mesa biome. The herobrine warrior built a bridge so that all creepers could pass through. While the warrior built the bridge, Steve hit the creeper behind him with his head. The creeper exploded and he was free. Then, he walked in the crowd made up of creepers, pretending he was being taken by a creeper. Then, Steve hit the creepers up front. About four creepers exploded, destroying the bridge and the warrior fell down. Then, as a bunch of creepers exploded and died, Steve freed Henry. "You won't get away like this!" the warrior yelled, as he fell down in the canyon.

"Never trust a griefer," said Steve. The sun rose as they crossed the canyon. When they made it to the mesa biome, they saw a chamber guarded with spiders and cave spiders. They could see herobrine warriors were they were standing. "More of Herobrine's warriors," said Henry. Steve saw that they were impacting. Then, explosions were heard through the sky "They are impacting for the destruction of the Overworld. No wonder the chamber is made of bedrock," said Steve.

They snuck upon the chamber. Cave spiders and spiders were guarding the entrance. Steve noticed the ground wasn't made out of bedrock. "I know a way to get in," said Steve. He started to dig a hole, looked at his compass, and dug in front of him, while crouching. Then, he dug up and found himself inside the chamber. There, nine herobrine warriors were crafting weapons and cooking food. Henry destroyed the spiders and Steve ignited a block of TNT and threw it at the warriors.

BOOM! The warriors were destroyed, and Steve along with Henry went deeper in the chamber. "I think they might be traps here," said Henry. "This is very similar to a temple." They searched the chamber for traps, but then, Steve stepped on a pressure plate. "Uh oh," said Steve. The ground opened and they fell into another room. Torches lighted up a huge hall way, like they were automatic.

Statues made out of clay stood in the spooky hall. They were crumbled up paper signs under the statues. "There's a statue of Notch," said Steve. "There's one of Jeb," said Henry. Famous players made out of statues were carved out of clay. A ghost-like scream echoed in the darkness of the huge room. *AHH!!* "What was that?" asked Steve nervously. They could see white eyes in the distance. Then, Steve found himself in an illuminated hall lighten by red stone torches. "Henry? Where are you?" asked Steve. Then, the ground broke. Steve fell into a burnt down village with zombies, and ghasts shooting at the villagers, destroying them.

"At last! The beginning of the Hostileworld!" yelled a sinister voice behind Steve. "NO!!" Steve cried, then, he found himself in a stronghold, and saw Notch being destroyed by a man with white eyes. "You will be destroyed!" the man said, then, Steve woke up in a stronghold. "Where am I? Was I dreaming?" asked Steve.

"You sure were," said Henry. They were stuck in a jail cell in a stronghold.

CHAPTER 4:
Sinister Plots

Herobrine emerged from a wall. "You two have been dumb enough to be caught. My herobrine warrior and my army of creepers have overwhelmed you," said Herobrine. Steve was dreaming! That's why he saw a creeper with a mechanical arm! It wasn't true. When the herobrine warrior threw the TNT when the creepers were chasing them, it must have some sort of sleepiness effects! He also remembered the statues! Were they- "Wake up, day dreamer!" Herobrine shouted to Steve. "I haven't slept in days," said Steve.

"You two are going to be my servants. You're going to destroy the world and join me in my army of hostile mobs," said Herobrine. "We will never betray the great army of Iron Golems," said Henry. "The '*Great Army of Iron Golems*'? Do you think your village is safe right now? My zombies are destroying them," said

Herobrine. "I do not believe you," said Henry. Herobrine walked over to Henry.

"Then what do you believe?" asked Herobrine. "I believe that we will stop you from taking over the Overworld and letting us out," said Henry, narrowing his eyes. "I don't believe you. Zombies!" yelled Herobrine. Two mutant zombies appeared from the corner. "Take these prisoners out. Lead them to the executions room. They will pay for treason," said Herobrine, angrily.

The mutant zombies had a strong grip and picked up Steve and Henry and picked them out of the jail cells. Herobrine led them to a huge room. Creepers, zombies, skeletons and spiders were watching them as they approached. There was a huge hole in the ground with blazes locked up. The mutant zombies threw them to the ice floor. BAM! "Release the blazes," said Herobrine.

Blazes flew out. Steve and Henry got their swords and battled the blazes. One blaze landed on the ground and hit Steve, and Steve got his sword and hit the blaze on the head, making the blaze flash red. Steve kicked the blaze and the blaze hit Steve again, damaging Steve. Steve got a potion of Fire Resistance and drank it, and destroyed the blaze instantly. Henry was having more trouble. He didn't take PvP classes like Steve, and he hit the Blaze on one of the rods. The blaze grew angry and shot fireballs at Henry, damaging him. The blaze shot another fireball, and without knowing, Henry deflected it.

Henry ran to the blaze and hit it on the face, and the blaze hit Henry again. Henry took out his diamond sword and hit the blaze, destroying it. A creeper walked to Herobrine. "This is too easy for them," hissed the creeper. "Do not worry, I have it all planned," said Herobrine. At a village that hadn't been destroyed, a girl named Alex was watching on a TV what was happening. She watched nervously how Steve and Henry fought.

The mesa biome was a few miles away, and she knew Herobrine as a foe, and she decided that Hostileworld should never come true. At the executions room, Steve encountered a ghast, and it shot a fireball at Steve. Steve deflected the fireball right back at the ghast, but he missed. Steve took out his fishing rod and aimed it at the ghast, and hooked it. He drew the ghast toward him and took out his sword and finished off the ghost. A wither skeleton lunged at Henry, infecting Henry. Steve ran over to help Henry, but a creeper jumped down and it exploded, blocking Steve's way.

Skeletons leaped down, firing arrows at Steve. Just then, someone approached Herobrine. "Stop right there, Herobrine," said a voice behind Herobrine. "Jeb Bergensten, you have crawled out of your hiding place," said Herobrine. "I'm not afraid of you, you monster," said Jeb. Herobrine took out a herobine sword and began battling Jeb. Jeb leaped up and took out a diamond sword and battled Herobrine. Down below, Steve and Henry were battling hostile mobs, trying not to get destroyed. Explosions boomed throughout the sky. Hostileworld was on its way to take over the Overworld.

Jeb clanged his sword against Herobrine's, and Herobrine flew upward and took out a Bow and Arrow. He shot dozens of arrows, and Jeb deflected them all. "You need teaching," Herobrine bragged, and shot fireballs at Jeb. Jeb jumped to avoid them, and a creeper snuck onto him. Jeb noticed the creeper and jumped as high as he could, and the creeper didn't explode. Just then, Alex arrived at the scene.

She took out an enchanted diamond sword and jumped at Herobrine, striking him. Herobrine noticed Alex and shot arrows, but missed. Ghasts went to aid Herobrine, as they shot fireballs, which distracted Jeb and Alex. Herobrine escaped and Steve and Henry were having trouble battling blazes. Jeb leaped down to help, not being damaged. Alex jumped down also, and they fought the blazes.

When the battle was over, Henry was surprised. "Who are you guys?" asked Henry. "My name is Alex," responded Alex. Jeb stood quiet. "Who are you?" asked Steve. The three looked at Jeb. "It's better if you do not know," said Jeb. "I overheard Herobrine say something about attacking the Ultimate City of Minecraft," continued Jeb. "If that means they are attacking... their attacking my village. Oh no!" cried Steve. Steve sprinted to get to his village.

"Steve, wait up!" cried Henry. Alex and Jeb followed. By midnight, explosions boomed through the sky as they reached the city. Steve watched in horror as fire spread, as zombies and the General Zombie destroyed the villagers. The Iron Golem army tried to defeat them, but the creepers blew them up. "We have to help them!" cried Steve, and ran to the village. He noticed Henry, Alex and Jeb weren't following him. "Come on! The villagers are in big trouble!!!" cried Steve.

"Steve, in some situations, you can't do anything. Take a look at that army. They will slobber us," said Henry. Henry stepped forward. *BOOM!* Explosions could be heard as the villagers were trying to evacuate. They ran into their burnt down houses, with horror filling them.

It was a new moon, with monsters everywhere. They were too late. Steve looked at his old burnt down house. He looked at the village being destroyed. Hostileworld was coming.

CHAPTER 5:
Steve's Plan

Flames light up the dark night as Steve watched his village get destroyed. Hordes of zombies destroyed every villager, every Iron Golem, while blazes and ghosts burnt down houses. Steve felt useless. Everyone felt useless. Steve had let his village down. Hostileworld was starting. Herobrine flew toward them.

"Too afraid? Well, you should be!" said Herobrine. "Although your army is powerful, you can never take over the world!" screamed Alex. "And what about you, Jeb?" asked Herobrine and he pointed at Jeb. "What?" asked Henry, shocked. "You have been hiding away too long, way too secret. You let down your world," said Herobrine. Jeb didn't say anything.

"Why are you doing this?" cried Jeb. "What are you talking about? I am Herobrine! Destined to destroy the world.

You will all be destroyed," said Herobrine and he took out a herobrine sword. Jeb, Steve, Henry and Alex took out their diamond swords. Herobrine charged at Jeb, and Jeb leaped over him. Herobrine hit Steve, taking 10 in damage. Alex leaped over Herobrine, hitting Herobrine from above. Jeb shot arrows, and Herobrine blocked the arrows with his sword.

Henry charged at Herobrine, hitting him, and Herobrine struck Henry with his sword. Jeb hit Herobrine, damaging Herobrine. Herobrine's sword clanged on Jeb's, making it harder for Herobrine to hit him. Steve charged at Herobrine, and Herobrine let go of Jeb and flew up again.

Steve shot arrows, and Herobrine blocked them with his sword. Herobrine flew down and Henry struck Herobrine, making Herobrine bleed. Alex was hit by Herobrine, and she began to bleed as well. Jeb charged at Herobrine with his diamond sword, but missed. "You nitwits have no idea how to face me. I got to your village by teleporting myself and my army. And that's what I'm going to now!" said Herobrine. He teleported away, along, with his army of hostile mobs. "That enemy doesn't know when to stop!" cried Steve, and he began to explode with hunger.

They walked to the village, wondering if anyone survived the attack. The sun rose and they expected to see villagers come out of the houses, but no one came out. Steve walked sadly to his old burnt down house. All his resources. His home. Everything was gone. His bed was destroyed. "I'm sorry Steve. This is what happens when you are in a huge fight," said Jeb. Alex and Henry searched for survivors, but there was no one at all.

"They are all gone," sobbed Steve. He looked at the village. He imagined villagers talking to each other. He imagined villagers picking crops and having ceremonies at the church. The Ultimate City of Minecraft, and it was gone. Steve could not believe Herobrine would do this. Anger boiled in him. He wanted revenge so badly, he wanted to destroy Herobrine. No wonder in his dream he saw him say that Hostileworld was coming.

Steve decided what to do. "We are going to the chamber that the herobrine warriors are impacting," said Steve as dozens of explosions exploded in the sky. "We can't," said Jeb. "Herobrine has a count down redstone powered clock that counts down to the destruction of the Overworld. It is inside the chamber surrounded by an energy field," continued Jeb.

"I'm going. Is anyone with me?" asked Steve. "I can't just stand here and watch the Overworld be destroyed, we will have to gather thousands of Iron Golems or archery villagers to defeat Herobrine," said Henry. "I am with you." "And so am I," said Alex. "Me too," said Jeb. Steve explained the plan to destroy Herobrine. "So, we are going o the remaining villages on the Overworld. Gather as many Iron Golems and archery villagers as you can. Henry, you do that. Alex, do you have a lot of friends?" asked Steve. "Certainly," said Alex. "Gather all of them. Jeb, you must sneak up on the chamber, too gather information about the clock or Herobrine," said Steve. "Consider it done," said Jeb. "Okay. Let's go stop Herobrine!" announced Steve.

Henry went to as many villages he could find. He gathered up to zero Iron Golems, and zero archery villagers. Herobrine has done serious havoc. Alex went to her village. She gathered about three friends. Jeb sneaked on the chamber. The count down was nine hours with fifty three minutes and nine seconds. He sneaked on from the back of the chamber, and saw a redstone repeater connected to about six pistons with a few activated levers that the pistons moved around to count seconds.

When they reunited, they shared everything. Steve had found a map that lead to the secret chamber. Alex's friends were named Christina, Lucy and Charlotte. "I have a map that leads to the chamber. It might take days to get there, but we need to stop Herobrine from taking over Minecraft," said Steve. "Then, we also must find Notch to get extra help." "Sounds like a plan," said Sophie. "Let's get started. Jeb, bring plenty of potions and healing," said Steve.

"I already have food and potions," said Jeb. "Okay. Let's get started," said Steve. They began heading east. As they walked it began to get dark. "Get your weapons out. No one is going to hold us off," said Steve. They headed toward an ocean. "Jeb, were crossing the ocean. Give us potions of water breathing," said Steve. As Jeb handed out potions, Steve could see a squid being zapped by tiny lasers.

"Do you see that?" asked Steve. They glanced at the squid being destroyed by a laser. "That's not natural," said Henry. "Guys were saving the Overworld here," said Sophie and she jumped in the water. The rest did, and soon, they found themselves in a water-like temple. "This isn't a good sign," said Christina. "There's an ocean monument," remarked Henry. They swam to get a closer look, but then suddenly a guardian appeared and shot a laser at Lucy. "Help!" she cried. Henry tried to swim toward her, but another guardian appeared and struck him with its spikes.

"Careful!" cried Steve, and swam toward Henry and Lucy. About six guardians appeared and charged at them, like tigers. "Swim up!" yelled Henry. They swam up and the guardians banged into each other. "Look out!" cried Steve. An elder guardian swam out of the fortress, ramming into Alex. "Help! I need to get away!" she cried. Jeb swam toward the elder guardian.

The elder guardian struck Jeb, and Jeb started to bleed. Steve swam to help Jeb, but a herobrine warrior appeared. "You aren't going anywhere. I have the monument filled," said the warrior. Henry swam toward the herobrine warrior, striking the warrior. "That's how you want to play? I will show you," said the warrior. The herobrine warrior swam toward Henry, and before he could hit him, Jeb blocked the warrior's sword. "You think you can face me?!" yelled the warrior. "You don't know a thing of who I am. I am the second player of Minecraft!" yelled Jeb. "What? Impossible. I thought the first players were dead!" said the warrior.

The warrior swam to Jeb, and hit him, making Jeb bleed. Jeb fought back hard, striking the warrior. Steve, Henry, Sophie, Christina and Lucy used this time to escape. Then, a guardian appeared. "Look out!" yelled Sophie, and the guardian stabbed Steve, Henry and Christina. They took out swords and hit the guardian as fast as they could.

They were getting tired. Jeb had all the food, but he was fighting outside the ocean monument. Then, an army of guardians charged at them. "Swim!" yelled Steve. They were in serious trouble. If they didn't make it out alive, who knows what will happen.

CHAPTER 6:
Jungle Beasts

As the guardians raced toward them, they tried to shoot arrows, but since they were underwater, the arrows didn't go far. "I have invisibility!" said Henry. He splashed it on the group. They turned invisible, and the guardians didn't know were they were. Then, they heard zombie groaning. They swam through water-covered halls to see what was making those groaning sounds.

Then, they saw a group of zombies that had their helmets enchanted with respiration. They talked to the guardians. "Steve and Henry have found a famous player. What do we do?" asked one of the zombies. "We ordered our boss, the elder guardian, do destroy them at all costs," said a guardian. "But they aren't three players anymore. They are six," said another guardian. The scuba zombies swam toward them, with their swords out.

Their invisibility was gone, and the scuba zombies saw them. Steve threw TNT to get them away. BOOM! "Get the gold out of here!" yelled the zombie general. Steve overheard them say 'gold.' Zombies had enchanted bows and arrows, and they shot at the group. "How can they shoot that far?!" cried Sophie. "Their bows are enchanted!" Steve noticed.

Jeb had defeated the herobrine warrior and headed inside the temple. As Steve, Henry, Christina, Sophie and Lucy swam to the exit; they were blocked off by an elder guardian. "Where do you think you guys are going?!" yelled the guardian. Two guardians appeared and took them to jail cells. "This is the second time! Leave us!" demanded Henry. Steve's water breathing effect was almost out.

Jeb was in the ocean monument, looking for them. But then, out of no were, the elder guardian appeared, seeing Jeb. "Where do you think you are going?" asked the guardian. "I am here to rescue my friends, you spiked up monster," said Jeb. "You will be destroyed," said the elder guardian. The elder guardian charged at Jeb, striking him with his spikes.

Jeb started bleeding on his head, and he swam toward the elder guardian, destroying three spikes. "You will never find my weakness!" yelled the elder guardian, charging to Jeb again. Jeb swam up, and the elder guardian missed him. The elder guardian shot a laser, and Jeb blocked it with his sword.

"I know your attack moves," said Jeb. "You will never manage to defeat me," replied the guardian. The guardian shot a slowness laser at Jeb, and Jeb stood still. The guardian shot harmful lasers at Jeb, hurting him so much he was close to being destroyed. At the jail cell, Steve was getting impatient. Then, he saw that a guardian had the key to the jail cell on its spike. Steve reached out for it, and snatched it.

"Good job," whispered Sophie. Steve freed himself and destroyed the guardian. "We have to get outside," said Lucy. "I know what we can do," said Christina. She explained her plan. As they talked, Jeb was battling the elder guardian. One spike went into Jeb's skin. Jeb started to bleed more. "You… won't get away with this," said Jeb. "Your words are weak, beginner," said the elder guardian.

Without knowing, Jeb escaped and trapped the elder guardian just by deflecting a slowness laser and drawing the elder guardian with a fishing rod in a jail cell. "You won't get away with this! My scuba zombies will aid me!" said the elder guardian. "Now your words are weak," said Jeb. Jeb went down the ocean monument and found Steve, Henry, Christina, Alex, Sophie and Lucy. "We must get out of here," said Alex.

As they made their way out, they approached the jungle. "Jungle's mean there might be an ancient temple," remarked

Christina. As they walked, they heard huge stomping. "Uh oh," said Henry. A tree was knocked down. Suddenly, six mutant zombies appeared stomping through the jungle like giants. "They see us! Run!" yelled Steve. They took shelter under a tree. The mutant zombies burnt down trees, like they were looking for something in the thick of trees.

"I wonder what they are up to," said Steve. As they burnt down a cluster of trees, the gigantic zombies looked around. "I think they are looking for a temple. What do you think, Jeb?" asked Alex. Jeb stood there and his face turned pale as snow. Steve looked in the direction Jeb was facing, and his jaw dropped. TNT explosions were in the air, and a huge fireball was approaching the Overworld.

Steve thought that Herobrine sent a huge fireball to destroy the Overworld. "What is that?!" cried Alex. A creepy mutant enderman was running, knocking trees down with its fists. A mutant creeper with five legs exploded and destroyed about four trees at a time. "Are they destroying the jungle?" wondered Henry. Steve saw the dangerous hostile mobs destroy the jungle, but then, Steve noticed some cobblestone in the distance.

"Wait a minute…" said Steve. Henry looked in the direction Steve was looking. "A temple!" he cried. "Shh!" hissed Sophie. It was too late. The mutant creatures charged at them, destroying about twenty blocks when they tried to hit them. The ground broke behind Steve, Jeb, Henry, Alex, Sophie, Christina and Lucy as the mutant mobs landed punches right behind them. "They can't see us though cobblestone! Come on!" said Alex. She led the group to the jungle.

Steve wanted this war to end. But when will it *really* end?

CHAPTER 7:
Notch is Back

They took cover in the jungle temple, and they thought they were safe. But someone awaits them at the deepness of the temple…

"Close one," gasped Lucy. The giant ferocious hostile mobs could not see them in the temple, so they were completely safe. "I must eat. It's been so long when we left my destroyed village," said Steve. "I have tons of food. Don't worry. All we have to do is beat Herobrine," said Jeb, as explosions could be heard in the sky. Steve sat down in the mossy ground of the temple.

Jeb handed out food to the group. Then, the group heard a sound of bones down in the chest room. "Skeletons. Herobrine must have sent them," said Henry. Steve took his sword out and raced to destroy the skeleton. But instead of seeing one, he saw a player that was half-skin-half-skeleton.

"What?!" said Steve. "I mean you no harm!" cried the half skeleton player. "I know that voice!" said Jeb and hurried down to Steve. The rest followed Jeb. "Who are… you players?" asked the half skeleton player. "I'm Steve. These are my friends Alex, Jeb, Christina, Lucy and Sophie," said Steve. "Jeb… that name sounds familiar," said the half-skeleton player.

Jeb stared at the skeleton player. Half of his body was gone, but on the other side, were tiny eyes and a huge beard with a brown shirt. "Notch?" asked Jeb. The skeleton player looked at Jeb. "You… know my name?" asked the skeleton player. "Are you really Jeb?" Jeb stood there quiet. "Wait, you are Notch! I'm Jeb!" said Jeb. "It can't be. I must be dreaming," said Notch. "This isn't a dream. Herobrine took over the Ultimate City of Minecraft and now taking over the Overworld," said Henry. Notch sat down on a moldy stone bench, with a nervous look.

"I knew Herobrine. He was a good friend. He was thrown into prison in a stronghold, and he was destroyed, turned into Herobrine," said Notch. "You never told me," said Jeb. "That was before I met you," said Notch. "I thought he was gone forever, but he isn't," said Notch.

"Besides the history stuff, can we hurry up?" Henry said. "The clock countdown is at six hours," said Christina. "You're right," said Alex. "Come on," said Steve. "I'm not going out there," said Notch. "What?" asked Jeb. "It is too dangerous. Ancient hostile mobs are on the prowl," said Notch. "Why are you staying here?!" cried Jeb. This time, Notch didn't say anything. "Come on! We have to hurry!" cried Steve.

Jeb took one last look at Notch, hoping he would be alright staying here. "You must go. They need you," said Notch. "Okay," answered Jeb. As they walked, they sneaked past the huge creatures. As they followed Steve's map, it got dark quickly when they reached the mesa biome. The red sand covered must of the biome. "There is the chamber," said Henry, pointing at it. *Just like in my dream* Steve thought.

Thousands of herobrine warriors were at the entrance. Steve didn't even know how many corridors they were. Thousands of cave spiders and spiders guarded the entrance. They secretly broke the energy field with a redstone circuit. "You have harmful potions?" asked Steve. "I sure do," responded Jeb, giving Steve a potion of Harming II. The chamber was on a hole in a cliff, so Steve climbed the cliff and splashed the spiders, destroying them,

"Stop right there, you thieves," said Henry as they took out swords to battle the herobrine warriors. "You won't get out of this alive, you foes," responded one of the herobrine warriors. "Herobrine has a hidden clock somewhere in the chamber. You will never find it!" said another warrior. "Oh yes we will!" said Alex, striking a warrior on the chest, making the warrior bleed. "Get them!" yelled a warrior. Six warriors charged at them, with diamond swords.

Steve was hit by a warrior, and started to bleed. Jeb leaped over a warrior and landed behind it, and destroyed it. But then, the zombie general along with other zombies appeared in battle. The zombies struck Jeb, making him bleed. Alex jumped over by a zombie, but the zombie general struck her as she jumped. Lucy went to help Alex, but she was hit too and started to bleed. "This is a loosing battle," said the warriors to the group. Sophie threw a potion of slowness on the warriors, and their pace began to slow and they got tired.

As the warriors filled their energy bar up, Steve, Jeb, Alex, Christina, Lucy and Sophie sneaked into the chamber, ready to find the clock hidden away in the corridors. "We may have to split up," said Jeb as they reached six corridors. Sophie took the first, Henry took the second, Steve took the third,

Lucy took the fourth, Alex took the fifth and Christina took the sixth. As Steve walked through the corridor, he sprinted through the icy corridor. The halls were made out of ice, making it harder for Steve to run.

Outside the corridor, Herobrine wondered why his warriors were outside eating his food. "What are you doing here? Go stop Steve, Henry, Alex and Jeb!" demanded Herobrine. "Sir, they aren't four. They are seven," said a warrior. "Seven? They just make themselves a bigger target. I'm taking your place to hunt them down," said Herobrine. Steve walked in the corridor, wondering if he would get lost in the thick of it.

Suddenly, a cluster of wind blew in front of him, and then Herobrine appeared. "Looking for my secret weapon? Not so fast!" Herobrine yelled. Herobrine took out his sword and Steve got his too. Herobrine charged at Steve, and Steve ducked under Herobrine, hitting his stomach, making Herobrine cry out in pain. "Is that how you want to play?!" yelled Herobrine. He threw his sword at Steve's face, making Steve bleed. Explosions could be heard throughout the sky. Steve charged at Herobrine ramming into him.

Herobrine swung his sword at Steve's face, missing to hit Steve. Steve was getting real, real tired of this. At a chamber nearby, Henry was battling two witches with a bow and arrow. One of the witches lunged at Henry, throwing a splash potion that damaged the witch and Henry. *Why would that witch throw a potion that would damage the witch and me?* Henry asked himself.

Sophie, Alex, Lucy and Christina were battling cave spiders. Steve, Henry, Alex, Jeb, Sophie, Lucy and Christina were all battling hostile mobs. But Steve had a boss to deal with. They all wondered where this would end. When will Herobrine be defeated?

CHAPTER 8:
Showdown

As Steve battled Herobrine, Herobrine was thinking the same thing. When would Steve and his friends be defeated? As they battled, Christina, Sophie, Lucy and Alex came running to the corridor Steve was battling. "We defeated the cave spiders!" said Christina. Herobrine shot an arrow at Christina, making her fall back. "I need back up!" cried Steve, covered in blood. His health was extremely low.

Suddenly, Jeb and Henry went to the corridor Steve was battling. "Herobrine! Stop right there!" yelled Henry, pointing at Herobrine. "You nitwits couldn't overpower me," said Herobrine. Herobrine exploded, and the blast threw the group outside the chamber. Steve was bleeding even more. "Run!" yelled Jeb. Herobrine sent ghasts and killer rabbits to destroy them. Fireballs struck the ground behind them as they ran.

"This is never ending!" cried Lucy. A killer rabbit was hitting Henry, as Henry was at the back of the group. Henry took out a diamond sword and destroyed the killer rabbit, and deflected the fireballs from ghasts. Fireballs hit the ghasts, which destroyed them. Gigantic mutated zombies appeared in front of them, and the zombie punched them, and the punch knocked the whole group back.

"My mutated zombies will never betray me!" said Herobrine. He took out a sword. Then, he took out some sort of communicator. "Launch the gigantic fireball down to the Overworld!" demanded Herobrine. "No!!!" cried Steve. He charged at Herobrine, but Herobrine flew up. The gigantic fireball smashed on the ground like a great fist, and there was a blast of hot red fire.

"It's happening!" sobbed Alex. The air was hot red. The group watched as the fireball hit the ground, destroying mountains, destroying villages, and the group could hear the last remaining villagers cry out in horror. Then, villages made out of red blocks replaced with regular ones. Villager's eyes turned white. Every NCP of Minecraft's eyes turned white. Hostileworld has come true. "You can't be doing this!" yelled Steve, and he cleaned out the blood from his face. Herobrine didn't respond. He landed and walked into the chamber. It was about eleven o'clock in the night. Tons of fire spread when mountains once were.

Steve looked at the group. "We are too late," he sobbed. Henry looked at Steve and stepped up. "I know we are too late. He was weak. We didn't know how to deal with Herobrine," said Henry. Lucy walked in front of Henry. "We can build a house to live in. Rather that Herobrine's ugly red ones," she said. Then, these memories appeared in Steve's mind. One was of him looking at the location of Jeb. One was from the executions room. Another memory when he was young and took PvP classes. Those three memories he had in his mind were very special. He could see them in his mind. But then, they slowly disappeared.

He felt like he had lost the war. He felt like he let down the whole history of Minecraft. He felt like he lost his villager friends. Everything he had built was gone. He dropped to the ground. Jeb was also sad as well. He wasn't able to protect them. Then, a skeleton player walked behind him. "You cannot change the past. You can change the future," said the skeleton player. Jeb recognized that voice. "Notch! You came to help!" Jeb cried happily.

"I decided I could not just stand there and watch you guys loose. I decided to step up," said Notch. Although he was old, he was a brave player. Steve's mind filled with bravery. "Come on. We are stopping Herobrine once and for all," he said. He led the group to the chamber. There, they saw the clock had reached zero. If they could destroy the red stone behind the clock, that would disable the fireball's destruction.

"Notch? Can you disable the clock?" asked Steve. "Of course I can," responded Notch. But before Notch could disable it, Herobrine appeared again. "What do you think you are doing?!!" yelled Herobrine. "We are going to stop your destruction of the Overworld!" said Steve, and he took out his diamond sword. Herobrine took out his sword. "Stop!" Notch called. "Notch?" asked Herobrine. "You are old. You cannot fight against me." "I may be old, but I can still fight," said Notch.

Herobrine charged at Notch with his sword pointed at him, and Notch dodged his attack, making Herobrine ram into a wall. Herobrine's sword was stuck on the wall. Quickly, Notch disabled the clock. "No! You will pay for this!" yelled Herobrine. He was furious. He punched Notch as hard as he could, and Notch started bleeding. Jeb leaped over and blocked Herobrine. Herobrine threw Jeb out of his way and struck Notch again. Henry leaped behind Herobrine, but Herobrine kicked Henry.

Lucy tried to strike Herobrine, but
Herobrine punched her back.

Steve could not just stand there seeing
the Creator get destroyed. It would be like in
his dream, he saw him get destroyed by
Herobrine. Suddenly, Steve leaped in front
of Herobrine and struck Herobrine with his
diamond sword. "You again!" said
Herobrine. "Yeah, I'm back!" said Steve. He
lunged at Herobrine and struck Herobrine.
Herobrine kicked Steve, and Steve took out
two diamond swords and charged at
Herobrine again. Herobrine summoned four
zombies, and Steve destroyed them
instantly. Notch ran over to help Steve, and
struck Herobrine again. Herobrine flew up
and avoided them. Henry, Lucy, Alex,
Christina and Sophie charged at Herobrine.

"You don't know when to stop, don't
you?" yelled Christina. "Get him!" said
Alex. The group charged at Herobrine.
Herobrine got his sword unstuck and flew
outside. Steve wasn't going outside, so he
got his enchanted bow and arrow with

harming II and shot Herobrine. Suddenly, Herobrine was shot by lightning nine times. It wasn't raining either. "NO!!!" cried Herobrine. Herobrine's eyes turned black and he disappeared.

Everything turned back to normal. Villages, mountains, and the burned ground turned back to grass. "What happened to Herobrine?" asked Sophie. "I have no idea," said Henry. They began building up the ground and they ate a ton of food.

"Me, Sophie, Christina and Lucy are heading out, okay?" Alex told the group. "Okay, we will write a letter," said Steve. "Me and Jeb are heading out too," said Notch. "Okay. I guess I will want to find a village for me to live in," said Steve. "I'm going with you. I'm technically homeless because I am an explorer," said Henry.

"Sure. Bye!" Steve and Henry waved to the rest. They were glad Herobrine was gone. They waved good-bye to their friends. Although hostile mobs still existed, they

have defeated the ultimate boss in
Minecraft.

Afterward...

Things were much better when Herobrine was destroyed. Villages remained peaceful and Iron Golems were well trained. Also, Herobrine was defeated in Minecraft 1.8.9, and that's why I decided to add this afterward part to tell you Herobrine was defeated in 1.8.9 so they removed Herobrine in Minecraft 1.9., and I call it: the Minecraft Legend (fan fiction).

Thank you for reading
-*Michael Rios*

46563269R00035

Made in the USA
Columbia, SC
24 December 2018